I HATE Weddings

I HATE Weddings

by P. J. PETERSEN

illustrated by LYNNE CRAVATH

DUTTON CHILDREN'S BOOKS • NEW YORK

Library of Congress Cataloging-in-Publication Data

Petersen, P. J.

I hate weddings / by P. J. Petersen;

illustrated by Lynne Cravath.—1st ed.   p.   cm.

Summary: When Dan has to meet his new stepfamily
and take part in his father's wedding, he finds that all sorts
of horrible and embarrassing things happen to him.

ISBN 0-525-46327-5 (hc)

[1. Weddings—Fiction. 2. Remarriage—Fiction. 3. Stepfamilies—Fiction.]

I. Cravath, Lynne Woodcock, ill.   II. Title.

PZ7.P44197 Iadw 2000   [Fic]—dc21   99-048165

Published in the United States by Dutton Children's Books,
a division of Penguin Putnam Books for Young Readers
345 Hudson Street, New York, New York 10014
www.penguinputnam.com/yreaders/index.htm

Designed by Alan Carr   ·

Printed in USA • First Edition

3   5   7   9   10   8   6   4   2

I HATE Weddings

Chapter ONE

I hate weddings. Big ones, little ones. They're all the same. Terrible.

To start with, I have to get dressed up. For me, that means my itchy blue suit. Then I'm supposed to sit still. No wiggling and no scratching. And we always get to the church about an hour early. So there's lots of time to sit on the hard benches and itch.

And weddings are kissy places. People run around kissing everybody. I hate that. Especially when they go after me. Women I hardly even know grab me and say, "Oh, Danny, I can't believe how much you've grown." And while I'm telling them my name is Dan, not Danny, they're laying a big old kiss on me. And leaving lipstick all over my cheek.

And everybody cries too. That's the dumbest thing of all. People are all happy, and they keep saying how beautiful everything is. But then they cry. And if you ask them what's the matter, they just shake their heads, like you're too stupid to understand. I hate that.

So here I was, on the airplane to Los Angeles, head-

3

ing for another wedding. And this was going to be the worst of all. I didn't just have to go; I had be *in* the wedding.

My dad was getting married. It was hard to get used to that idea. For years Dad had lived by himself in neat apartments. Now he was marrying Joan, this woman I'd only met one time. And he'd be moving into her house. And Joan had two kids I'd never even seen.

The whole thing was creepy. I tried not to think about it. I tilted my seat back and tried to enjoy the flight. It was one of only two good things about the weekend. (The other was missing school on Friday.)

I liked flying by myself. I got to do it every two or three months. I flew from my home in San Francisco to Los Angeles (Burbank Airport) to spend the weekend with Dad. That was our time. We always went to fun places like Dodger games and the beach, and we played ball and went swimming.

I always got a window seat. I like to look out and try to guess where we are. And when you're a kid flying alone, you sometimes get extra peanuts and extra Cokes.

I usually like talking to the people around me. But not this time. I kept my face turned toward the window. The first thing people ask is where you're going and why. And what could I say? I'd have two choices—both bad.

One choice was to make up something. Maybe say I was going to Disneyland or Universal Studios. Dad and I had done those things before. But it wouldn't work. I'm a terrible liar. I might as well have a sign on my forehead that flashes LIE! LIE! Even little kids know when I'm not telling the truth. And my mother can spot a lie before I get my mouth open.

But the other choice was to tell the truth. And what if I did that? What if I smiled and said, "I'm going to my dad's wedding"? Right away people would start feeling sorry for me. I hate that.

If you like to get dippy looks, just tell people your mom and dad are divorced. People don't pat you on the head and say, "Poor little boy." But they might as well.

It's dumb for people to feel sorry for me. I can't even remember when Mom and Dad were together. I've always lived with Mom. Dad comes to see me when he can. And now that I'm older, I get to go see him sometimes. That's the way things are, and it's what I'm used to. But people don't see it that way.

When I told Ms. Crane, my teacher, why I'd be

gone on Friday, she gave me one of those looks. Then she said, "How do you feel about your father getting married again?"

I hate that kind of question. It's hard to explain how you feel. Even if you want to. Which I didn't. So I just said, "Fine." And I got another look.

The flight was bad. We were in clouds most of the time. That gave us a bumpy ride, and I couldn't see the ground. And I only got one little glass of Coke that was mostly ice. For once, I was glad when we came in for a landing.

When our plane stopped at the gate, I grabbed my backpack from under the seat. All I had in it was a book and a cassette player. My clothes, including my itchy blue suit, were in my suitcase. And I had checked that. Usually I worried about checking my bags. Not this time. If they lost that itchy blue suit, that was okay with me.

I came up the ramp and through the door. The terminal was hot and noisy. People were crowding all around. I could barely squeeze past all the people hugging and kissing. I walked through the crowd, expecting to see Dad any second. He always got close to the door.

But I didn't see him.

I slowed down and looked around. I saw lots of huggers and kissers. Men with briefcases pushed past me.

I ended up by a wall. I felt funny standing there, like nobody wanted me. I felt like Dickie Moore, this kid who gets picked last whenever we choose sides for baseball.

I couldn't believe I'd missed Dad. That had never happened before. I turned around and started back toward the gate. That wasn't easy. Everybody was headed the other way, and I kept getting banged with suitcases and elbows.

When I finally got to the door, the last of the people were coming out. I stood and looked around. Dad wasn't there.

A woman in a blue uniform came over to me. "Are you all right?"

"No problem," I said, and headed away from her.

I don't know why I did that. I should have told her the truth. But I didn't. Instead, I turned around and moved along with the crowd.

When I saw a telephone, I stopped. I used my calling card to call Dad's apartment. After a bunch of clicks and beeps, a robot voice said, "The number you have dialed is no longer in service." I knew that was wrong. But how can you argue with a robot?

I dug in my wallet for Dad's cell-phone number. I

punched in those numbers and felt better when I heard the first ring. But nobody answered. I hung up after twenty-two rings.

I walked back toward my gate. The areas around other gates were jammed with people, but mine was empty. I stood by the wall and looked around.

I knew something must have happened. Dad wouldn't forget me. But then I started thinking about dumb things. Like Dad going to the wrong gate. Or the wrong airport. Or Dad getting in a wreck. Or having somebody steal his car. Really dumb things. But I couldn't help it.

I spotted a candy machine. It took me two seconds to decide I needed a candy bar. I was hungry, and I might be at the airport for a long time.

The candy bar, which I could buy at a store for fifty cents, cost a dollar. That took almost all of my change.

I sat in a chair by the gate and put my backpack in the next chair. Things were really quiet. I decided to make my candy last a long time. I checked my watch, then looked at the candy bar. I could get eight bites out of the candy. If I took a bite every fifteen minutes, the candy would last two hours.

That was a good plan. But it didn't work. I started thinking about dumb things again, and suddenly the

candy bar was gone. I checked my watch. The candy had lasted four minutes.

I was still hungry. I dug into my pocket and pulled out every last coin. I had thirty-eight cents.

I had two twenty-dollar bills in my wallet. But they were no good for the candy machine. I had to get change. I grabbed my backpack and moved to the center of the walkway. I could see some kind of store down at the end. But it was a long way from the gate.

Dad would probably be coming any minute. I'd better stay where I was. For a little while anyway.

I looked over at the phones and thought about calling Mom in San Francisco. But what could she do? And I didn't want her worried.

I sat and tried not to look at my watch. But that's like trying not to think about candy. So I decided to play a game. I'd see how long I could go without checking the time. I decided to count so that I wouldn't start thinking about dumb things again. I was up to four hundred before I lost count.

I glanced at my watch. Two minutes, ten seconds. I thought my watch must be broken.

I spotted the woman in the blue uniform. I grabbed my book out of the backpack and held it in front of my face.

She stopped right in front of me, but I kept my eyes on the book. "Is everything all right?" she asked.

"Sure," I said.

"Are you waiting for someone?"

I didn't want to get in trouble. I just wanted her to go away. "I'm waiting for my mother," I said. "She's in the rest room."

I thought that would take care of things. But I'm no good at stuff like that. The woman didn't believe me for a minute. I could tell. She gave me a quick smile and said, "You came in on Flight two-fifty-seven, didn't you? What's your name?"

"Dickie Moore," I said, using the first name that came to me.

"Hi, Dickie," she said. "I'm Megan."

I smiled and said hi. She looked me straight in the eye, and I ended up looking down at my feet.

"Dickie," she said after a minute, "which way did your mother go?"

I kept looking at my feet. I was stuck. I wanted to quit the stupid lying. But I couldn't figure out what to say.

"Dickie?" she said again. "Which way did she go?"

Chapter TWO

I kept staring at my feet. I was ready to tell the truth. But I couldn't figure out where to start.

Then I heard footsteps, and a little boy came running toward us. "Hey, Dan," he shouted, "we're here."

The woman looked at him, then back at me. "Dan?" she said.

Dad came rushing up to us. "I'm sorry, Dan," he said, breathing hard. "There was an accident on the freeway. We didn't move for an hour. And I went off without my cell phone." He put his hand on my shoulder. "I hope you weren't worried, buddy."

"No problem," I said.

"We ran all the way from the parking lot," the boy said.

Dad smiled at the woman. "Thank you for looking after him."

"You're welcome." The woman gave me a funny look, then said, "Say hi to your mom for me, Dickie." And she walked away.

"What was that about?" Dad asked me.

I shook my head. "We were playing a game."

The little guy gave me a push and held out his hand. "I'm Riley," he said. "Give me some skin, big guy."

I started to shake his hand, but I could see he wanted something more. So I slapped his hand twice. "Hey, Riley," I said.

Riley smiled. "Were you scared? Getting off the plane and not seeing anybody?"

"I knew you'd come," I said.

"I woulda been scared," Riley said. "I woulda been really scared. I woulda yelled."

Dad put his arm around me. "I'm sorry, buddy. That's terrible—standing around and wondering what went wrong."

"No problem," I said.

"How was your flight?" Dad asked me.

"Okay. A little bumpy."

"You know what happened to me?" Riley said. "I was on a plane one time, and it was bouncing all over the place. I got sick and threw up in a bag." He giggled. "But I missed the bag with some of it."

The three of us walked through the terminal. Riley kept looking up at me and smiling. "We're gonna be brothers," he said. "Isn't that neat?"

We went downstairs and got my suitcase and took it to Dad's car. "Hey, Dan," Riley said, "we can sit in the backseat."

I looked up at Dad, and he winked at me. "Sure," I said.

Once we got going, Riley started telling me stupid jokes like "What did the dog say when he sat on sandpaper?" (The answer, in case you care, is "Ruff.") And he told me about his best friend, a guy named Paul, who was always getting into trouble.

"Paul hides behind a bush with the water hose," Riley said. "He waits for people to drive by in a convertible with the top down. Then he lets them have it."

"Are you sure this was Paul?" Dad asked. "I thought maybe Riley was doing that."

Riley laughed. "I wouldn't do it. And we don't have the right kind of thing on our hose." He grabbed my arm. "You know what happened to Paul? He squirted this woman on a bicycle, and she stopped and grabbed the hose and soaked him."

A little later Riley started bouncing up and down. "This is so neat," he said. "This is soooooo neat."

"What?" I said.

"I'm gonna have a big brother." He laughed out loud. "My friend Sam's got a big brother, and his big brother takes him to ball games and teaches him to throw the Frisbee and all kinds of stuff." Riley looked over at me. "And sometimes his big brother gives him gum."

"I don't have any gum," I said.

Riley laughed and pointed at Dad. "I know somebody that does. Sugarless. The kind my mom lets me have. But Mom says I'm not supposed to ask him for gum."

Dad reached back and handed us a pack of gum. "How'd you know I had gum in my pocket?" he asked.

Riley laughed. "I just did."

I handed him the pack. "Here you go."

He took a piece, stripped off the paper, and popped it into his mouth. "Thank you, big brother."

"You're welcome, little brother."

I felt great. I'd been a little worried about Dad's new family. If they didn't like me, I might not get to come here to visit Dad. But Riley was already my buddy.

"You get to stay at my house," Riley said. "In my room. Isn't that neat?"

"I think I'm staying with Dad," I said. That was one of the good things about visiting Dad. I got to sleep on his couch in the living room. Right next to a big TV with a satellite dish that got hundreds of channels. I loved it—monster movies, *Roadrunner* cartoons, microwave popcorn, and me on the couch with a remote.

"I wish you could," Dad said. "But things are a mess here. I was just going to tell you about it. I've sold my furniture, and my other stuff is in Riley's garage. So you really can't stay at my place."

Riley punched my arm. "He's moving into our house. Isn't that neat?"

"But couldn't I—"

Dad shook his head. "I'm sorry, buddy. Everything is crazy right now."

"I could sleep on the floor," I said.

"Not this time," Dad said.

"Don't you want to stay with me?" Riley asked, looking really sad.

"Sure." What else could I say?

"I have bunk beds," Riley said. "You can have the top or the bottom. Whatever you want. You could sleep with me, but I wiggle a lot. One time when we were on vacation, I had to share a bed with Uncle Tony. He said I kept jabbing him and poking him all night. He said it was like sleeping with a porcupine."

At Riley's house Dad got my bag out of the trunk.

Riley grabbed the bag, carried it up the steps, and threw open the door. "Mom," he yelled, "Dan's here. And he's really cool."

I tucked in my shirt and ran my fingers through my hair. I wanted to get off to a good start.

Dad and I walked up the steps. "I'm glad you're here, buddy," Dad said.

I felt really funny right then. This was the house where Dad was going to live. With a new wife. And a new family.

Joan met us at the door. She looked different from the way I remembered her. I wasn't sure why. "Come in, Dan. It's good to see you again."

"Hi," I said.

"Let's go, Dan," Riley called. "I'll show you my room."

Joan came toward me with her hand out. I reached out and took her hand. As soon as I did that, I saw her other hand. She had been coming to hug me. And I, like a dope, ended up shaking her hand.

Joan took my hand in both of hers. "I'm so glad you could come. We wanted you here for the wedding."

I couldn't think of anything to say. Not one thing. I just stood there with a stupid smile on my face. I knew she must think I was a real loser.

A girl rushed past me and hugged Dad. "You got here just in time. I have a math problem that I can't figure out. And neither can Mom."

"And this is Hannah," Joan said.

Hannah was about my size. She was probably only a year or two older than I was. But it seemed like ten years. Her dark hair was short but fancy. She was wearing jeans and a UCLA sweatshirt, but she looked dressed up. "Hi," she said, looking down at my feet.

"Hi."

"Where do you find green shoelaces like that?" Hannah asked. "I've never seen them before." She made them sound really stupid.

I hadn't even thought about my shoes. All the kids at my school wear bright green laces. "They give them to us at my school," I said. "Green and white are our school colors."

"How cute." She rolled her eyes up so far they almost went out of sight.

"Let's go, Dan," Riley called.

"Just a minute," Dad said. "Dan needs to call his mother."

Joan showed me the phone. Hannah brought her math book to Dad, and they sat on the couch with it. I punched in my calling card number and then our

number. After two rings, the answering machine came on. I heard my own voice saying we couldn't come to the phone right now. Except it didn't sound like me. "Mom," I said after the beep, "I got here fine. Everything's fine. Bye."

"You didn't have to use your calling card," Joan said.

"That's why Mom got it for me," I said. "So I could make long-distance calls from a stranger's house."

As soon as the word *stranger* came out, I knew it was the wrong word. A funny look passed over Joan's face, but then she smiled again.

"That was so easy, Mom," Hannah said. She closed her book and stood up. "I was multiplying when I should have been dividing."

"Nothing to it," Dad said. "Not for us brainy types."

"I'm glad something was easy," Joan said. "This has been one of those days. We almost didn't have a cake. And the organist hurt her hand." She smiled at me. "Have you been to many weddings, Dan?"

I almost said, Too many. The way I see it, even one wedding is too many. But I caught myself in time and said, "Some."

Joan kept looking at me like she expected me to say

more. I stood there for a long time, then said, "I went to one two weeks ago."

"That's good," Joan said. "Then you know what to expect."

"That one was different," I said. "Weird. It was a lot of talking. Not the regular stuff."

Joan smiled. "You didn't like that?"

"It was kind of dumb," I said. "They had all this extra stuff. Like he'd call her if he was late. And she'd get regular exercise. And he'd help the kids with their homework. And go to their soccer games."

"What's dumb about that?" Hannah asked me.

"Doesn't sound dumb to me," Dad said.

"It was," I said. "Really dumb."

Joan took Dad's hand and smiled at him. I was pretty sure I'd said something stupid. But I didn't know what.

"You can put your things away," Joan said. "Then we'll have something to eat."

"Come on, Dan," Riley said. He was still holding my bag. "My arm's about to break."

I went with Riley. Behind me, I heard Hannah say, "Mom, did you see those shoelaces?"

"Shh," Joan whispered.

Chapter THREE

Riley's room was great. The walls were covered with posters of animals and airplanes. The bedspreads had pictures of rockets. And, best of all, there weren't any girls in there.

"I had to clean it before you came," Riley said.

"It looks good," I said. I opened my suitcase and got out my itchy blue suit. I had promised Mom I'd hang it up right away.

"I threw all the junk into the closet and shut the door." He slid open the closet door and showed me a big pile of toys and clothes. There were some old French fries mixed in.

I hung my suit off to the side so the bottom of it wouldn't touch Riley's pile. "I can't get away with that," I told him. "My mom always checks the closet."

"My mom doesn't come into my room," Riley said. "She doesn't like Melvin."

"Who's Melvin?"

"He's over there." Riley pointed at a fish tank sitting on his dresser.

I came closer, expecting to see a fish. But I realized there was no water in the tank. On the bottom were rocks and some sticks.

Then I saw Melvin. A big hairy spider. Really big. He looked like he'd eat rats for breakfast. I'd never seen anything uglier in my whole life.

"He's a tarantula," Riley said. "Isn't he neat?"

"Yeah," I said. "He's the biggest one I ever saw."

Riley lifted up the screen on top of the tank and reached inside. "You can hold him."

I stepped back, ready to run. "I better not."

"You aren't scared of spiders, are you, big brother?" Riley lifted the giant spider out of the cage.

"No way," I said. "I just don't want to scare *him*. Spiders are kind of bashful. They get scared around strangers."

Riley petted the spider. "It's okay, Melvin. This is my big brother." He looked over at me. "Did you ever have a pet tarantula?"

"No," I said. "I wanted one, but—"

"I'll bet I know. I'll bet your dad wouldn't let you have one. He's scared of 'em. I didn't know that. I ran up and showed Melvin to him, and he got all white in the face. He had to sit down and put his head between his knees. I didn't mean to scare him."

"Melvin's pretty big," I said. "Lots of people would be scared of him."

Riley laughed. "Hannah's scared of him. She's really scared. She won't even look at him. And Mom makes me take him outside when she changes my sheets. But we think he's neat, don't we, big brother?"

"Right."

"You want to take him now?"

"We'd better let him get used to me. Let him see me for a day or two. Then he won't be nervous." And by then I'd be on my way back home.

Riley put Melvin back in the glass tank. "You want the top bunk or the bottom?" he asked.

"Where do you usually sleep?"

"On top," Riley said. "I used to be scared of having monsters under the bed. So I slept up on top where they couldn't get me. But you can sleep there if you want."

"I'll take the bottom," I said. "I'm not scared of monsters."

"I know that," Riley said. "You're big. You're prob'ly not scared of anything."

I didn't answer that one.

Riley opened his desk drawer and showed me his rock collection, a silver dollar, and a package of balloons. "Uncle Tony gave me the balloons," he said. "When summer comes, I'm gonna fill them up with water. Then when Hannah is sunbathing out in the backyard, POW! Maybe you can come and visit me, and we'll both get her."

I liked the idea, but I didn't say so.

Riley took a picture out of the drawer and handed it to me. "You know who this is?"

It was a picture of a man standing by a car. I'd never seen him before. "No."

"That's my other dad. He lives in Oregon, and I don't see him much. Your dad's lots better. He takes me places and tells me jokes and stuff."

Then he showed me his stack of baseball cards. "Uncle Tony gave me these. He's really neat. He has an earring, and he plays the drums, and he goes to San Diego State. He used to stay with us sometimes." Riley looked over at me and whispered. "He'd get in big fights with his stepdad, and he'd come live with us for a while."

We went back to the kitchen. On the table was a plate of carrots and celery. No cookies. No chips. Just like home—darn it. Why couldn't Dad marry somebody who liked cookies and candy and junk food?

"Have you ever had aronia juice?" Joan asked me.

"No," I said.

"It's good," Riley said.

Hannah filled red plastic glasses with purple juice and handed them to Riley and me. "Thank you," I said, hoping that Joan noticed.

Hannah gave me a funny smile. "You're welcome."

I raised my glass and took a sip. I felt something cold on my chest. Purple juice was dripping onto my shirt. I pulled the glass away from my mouth. It kept dripping. I grabbed a napkin and wrapped it around the glass. "This thing leaks," I yelled.

Riley laughed. "You had an accident."

"It's okay," Joan said, taking a sponge from the sink. "I'll take care of it."

I didn't want her to think I was a slob. "There's something wrong with the glass," I said.

Joan took the glass and the soggy napkin from my hand. She set them in the sink, then came back and mopped the table.

Dad reached into the sink and picked up the glass. "It has a hole in it," he said. Like that was big news.

"I told you," I said.

"Oh, I'm so sorry," Joan told me. "I'll wash that shirt for you. I hope it isn't stained."

"Don't worry about it," Dad said. That was easy for

him to say. He wasn't standing there with a sopping wet, purple shirt.

"I'm so sorry," Joan said again. "This has been one of those days. One thing after another."

I glanced over at Hannah. She had this nasty smile on her face. Maybe Dad and Joan thought the leaky glass was an accident. Hannah and I knew better.

Joan poured me another glass of juice. I smiled and took some carrot sticks.

Riley let out a yelp. "Uh-oh, I had an accident." I looked over and saw purple juice dribbling down his shirt. He laughed out loud. "Now we're twins, big brother."

For dinner we had stir-fry. Dad was supposed to have dinner with the men in his office, so he just sat at the table with us. But he kept eating things from our plates. "I can't help it," he said. "It looks too good."

Joan finally got him a plate.

"I'll just have a little," he said. But he ate more than anybody.

I was really careful at the table. I wanted Joan to see that I wasn't really a slob. But things still went wrong.

At home I never drop anything. But at Joan's

house, when I was trying to do everything right, food kept falling off my fork. And as soon as I got a big mouthful, Joan would ask me a question.

And every time I had a problem, Hannah would elbow Joan to be sure she noticed.

Afterward, Dad played a game called Tiddlywinks with Riley, Hannah, and me. "You guys are in trouble," Dad said. "I've been practicing."

"He's no good," Riley whispered to me.

Dad laughed. "I heard that. But things are different now. I have a new way to shoot."

I had never played Tiddlywinks before, and I was lousy at it. But Dad was worse. "I've got it figured out," he'd say. "It's all in the timing. Here comes my perfect shot." Then he'd shoot a wink clear off the table.

We laughed and laughed. Even Hannah.

When Dad had to leave, he hugged everybody and said, "I'll tell you a secret. I let you guys win."

After Dad left, things were different. Right away Hannah picked up a book the size of an encyclopedia. Riley wanted to play this baby game called Candyland, so I played it with him. Hannah sat on the couch and pretended to read her book. But she was watching me the whole time.

"This is so neat," Riley said to her. "We're getting a new brother."

Hannah snorted. "With a brother like you, do you think I need another one?"

I was feeling cheated. All week I had been picturing myself on Dad's couch, watching monster movies. Instead I was playing boring old Candyland and getting rotten looks from Hannah.

"Whipped you again, big brother," Riley said, slapping hands with me. "Good try."

"You're Candyland champion," I said.

"It's time for bed, Riley," Joan called from the kitchen. "We have a big day tomorrow, and you're already an hour later than usual."

"Can't we stay up and see Uncle Tony?" Riley asked. "Please."

"He won't be in until late," Joan said.

"That's okay," Riley said. "We're not sleepy."

"It's bedtime," Joan said again.

I was hoping for a snack. At dinner I'd been so careful about my manners that I hadn't eaten much. Now after looking at candy for four games, I was starving. I'd eat anything—even healthy stuff. But nobody mentioned food.

I gathered up the pieces to the Candyland game while Riley ran out to the kitchen. "Was that fun?" Hannah asked me. "Or was that game too hard for you?" That was supposed to be a joke, I guess.

"Give me a break," I said. "What are you reading?"

She gave me a snotty look and held up the big book. "*Mammals of North America.*"

I'd never heard of it before, but I said, "Oh, yeah. I read that last year. It was pretty good."

That stopped her for a second. She probably didn't believe me, but she couldn't be sure.

"Let's go, big brother," Riley called.

I carried the Candyland game to the kitchen, hoping it might give Joan some ideas. But she was sitting at the table, going over a list. She looked up at me. "I'm glad you could come, Dan," she said. "It means a lot to your father."

"I like coming to see him," I said. Then I realized how that sounded. I should have said I was glad to come to the wedding. Or something like that. But it was too late.

"You don't have to go to bed right now," Joan said. "Riley has to go to school tomorrow, but—"

"That's okay," I said. "I'm pretty tired." I'd said

and done enough dumb things for one day. I couldn't get to Riley's room fast enough.

"Dan likes Melvin," Riley told her.

"That's nice," Joan said. She stood up and hugged Riley. "Good night, honey."

Then Joan turned to me. I saw that she was going to hug me, but I was holding the Candyland box. I looked around for somewhere to put it, then stepped back and set it by the stove.

"That's all right, Dan," Joan said. "I won't hug you."

What could I say to that? She thought I was moving away from her. And I didn't know how to explain that she was wrong. So I just stood there like a dope.

I'd been doing a lot of that lately.

Chapter FOUR

"Y̶ou want to kiss Melvin good night?" Riley asked me.

"I don't like kissing," I said.

"Me neither," Riley said. "And his legs tickle my nose."

I dug through my suitcase. After I'd been through everything three times, I told Riley, "I forgot my pajamas."

"I have extras," Riley said. He hauled some Mickey Mouse pajamas out of his dresser.

I held the bottoms in front of me. The legs came just below my knees. "Not my size," I said. "That's okay. I'll just sleep in my underwear."

"Me too," Riley said. "You know what Paul and I do sometimes? We get under the covers with a flashlight, and we play Candyland."

"I'm pretty tired," I said.

Riley reached into the fish tank and patted Melvin. "Good night, Melvin."

"Where did you get him?" I asked.

"Dad gave him to me. Not your dad. My other dad. He came by for a visit, and we went to the mall. We saw Melvin in a pet store. Our class was studying spiders right then, so Dad bought him for me. He knew Mom wouldn't like him, so he told me not to tell her until he was gone."

"What did your mom say?"

Riley laughed. "She was mad. Real mad. She wanted to take Melvin back to the store, but I begged and begged. And then the store wouldn't take him back. So Mom made me a deal. I got to keep Melvin, but she wouldn't come into my room. I have to do all the work in here."

I looked at the pile of clothes in the closet, but I didn't say anything.

Riley flipped off the overhead light and turned on a night-light. "I'm not scared of the dark. I just like a little bit of light. In case I have to go to the bathroom or something."

I got into the bottom bunk, and Riley went up the ladder. "This is neat," he said. "My big brother right here in my room."

"Good night, Riley," I said.

"Good night, big brother." Then he giggled. "Good

night, Melvin. Good night, closet. Good night, window. Good night, door."

"That's enough, little brother," I said.

"You know what Paul did?" Riley said. "He stayed overnight here, and he wanted to sleep in the top bunk. He got a glass of water and waited until I was almost asleep. Then he reached down and dripped some water on me. And he told me he wet the bed and that was what was dripping down."

"Good night, Riley."

"Good night, Dan. Good night, Melvin. Good night—" He went on and on, but I didn't say anything. Pretty soon he asked, "Are you asleep?"

"Yes," I said.

"Then how come you're talking?"

"I talk in my sleep."

Riley giggled. "Good night, Dan. Good night, Melvin. Good night—"

I was really tired, but I couldn't get to sleep. I kept thinking about all the dumb things that had happened with Joan. She had to figure I was a real loser.

And I thought about Dad and how he'd be here playing Tiddlywinks with his new family while I was back home in San Francisco.

I lay on one side for a while. Then on the other side. Then I lay on my back and looked around the room. The night-light made everything look creepy. I thought about Melvin in his tank. I hoped the top was on tight.

My empty stomach was making noises. I started thinking about good things to eat. Not healthy stuff. Candy bars and pizza and potato chips and doughnuts.

"Hey, Riley," I whispered.

No good. He'd finally gone to sleep.

I got out of bed and went to the door. I listened for a minute, then tiptoed down the hall to the bathroom.

When I came back into the hall, I thought about that purple juice. Even that would taste good.

I stopped for a second and looked toward the kitchen. I could see light out there, but I didn't hear anything.

I couldn't stand it. I had to have something to eat. Otherwise I'd never get to sleep.

I tiptoed into the kitchen and looked around. The only light came from the family room. The couch in there had been made into a bed, but nobody was in it.

I opened the refrigerator. That made more noise than I expected. I stood still and listened for a minute. Then I looked inside for the juice. I took out the bottle and saw there was only a little bit left. I didn't want to finish the bottle, so I put it back.

There had to be something in that refrigerator. I opened the bottom drawer, hoping for some good fruit. All I saw was broccoli and cabbage and mushrooms.

I opened the freezer compartment. Right in front was an ice cream carton. I grabbed it and looked at it in the light of the refrigerator. Blueberry swirl yogurt. Not my first choice maybe. But a whole lot better than broccoli.

I knew where the silverware drawer was. I opened it and grabbed a big spoon. I didn't need an ice-cream scoop.

But I needed a bowl. I tried two cabinets, then decided to go with what I had.

I went over to the sink and dug out a big scoop of yogurt. Leaning over the sink, being careful not to drip, I ate it off the spoon. Delicious.

One spoonful wasn't enough. I had to have one more.

I'd been eating off that spoon, though. I couldn't put it back into the yogurt. So I turned on the faucet and let the water run until it was good and hot. Then I washed the spoon very carefully.

I dug into the yogurt again. The warm spoon

worked better, and I got a much bigger scoop that time.

But when I lifted out that scoop, it slid off the warm spoon and plopped onto the floor.

I wanted to cry. I looked around for some paper towels, but I couldn't see any.

Then I heard a noise in the hallway. Joan called, "Tony, is that you?"

I couldn't move. I stood there in the middle of the kitchen and stared toward the hall.

"Tony?" Joan called again. I heard her footsteps coming toward the kitchen.

I couldn't let her see me. Not in my underwear. I dropped to my knees and crawled under the table. I scooted up against a chair and held my breath.

Joan flipped on the light. Crouching where I was, I could only see her from the waist down. That meant she couldn't see me. I hoped.

"What's this?" She must have seen the yogurt carton. I watched her bare feet walk across the floor to the sink.

I saw the trouble coming before it happened. Her feet were headed right for the scoop of yogurt. I wanted to yell and warn her. But nothing would come out of my mouth.

Her bare foot clomped down right in the middle of

the yogurt. She screamed and jumped back. Then she muttered something and hopped on one foot over to the sink.

She bent over and used a towel to wipe off her foot. When she did that, her head was low enough to see me there under the table. She let out a noise and jumped again. Then she leaned against the cabinets and looked at me. "Dan?"

I didn't say anything. What do you say to your new stepmother when she finds you hiding under the kitchen table in your underwear?

Joan didn't seem to know what to say either. She wiped her foot, then looked at me. Then wiped her foot some more. "I hope," she said after a while, "that there's a good explanation for this."

"I don't think so," I said.

"Maybe you ought to come out from under there."

I looked down at my bare legs. "I forgot my pajamas," I said. "I had to sleep in my underwear."

Joan wiped her foot again, then straightened up so that I couldn't see her face.

I waited a long time for her to say something. Then I said, "I'm sorry." My voice was all squeaky.

"I'll tell you what," she said quietly. "I'll go back to bed. You clean up everything. Is that a deal?"

"It's a deal," I said.

It took me a long time to get the floor clean. I made sure there was nothing sticky anywhere. Then I put the yogurt carton back in the freezer without taking another taste.

I wasn't hungry any longer.

Chapter FIVE

The first thing I heard Friday morning was Riley scooting down the ladder. "Gotta go, gotta go," he whispered. He ran out the door and down the hall.

I looked at my watch: six-thirty. I rolled over and pulled the covers around my ears.

Riley came back into the room and plopped down beside me. "I almost had an accident," he said. "I'm lucky I woke up right then." He giggled. "You're lucky, too, big brother. You were right under me."

"Maybe you should go back to bed," I said.

Riley laughed. "It's morning. We don't want to sleep anymore."

"I'm pretty tired," I said.

"Maybe I could get in with you," Riley said. "That might help me sleep."

It was worth a try. I scooted to the far side of the bed, and Riley crawled under the covers. "This is nice and warm," he said. He was quiet for about ten seconds. Then he said, "Dan?"

"Go back to sleep."

"I want to ask you something."

"We can talk later."

"Please. Just one thing."

I rolled over and looked at him. "What is it?"

Riley smiled. "What's your middle name?"

"Edward," I said. "Now go to sleep." I turned my back to him and put the pillow over my head.

Riley laughed. "You're grumpy in the morning. So is Hannah. If you say anything to her, she'll bite your head off. Mom's not quite so grumpy. She just doesn't like to talk much until she has some coffee."

I lay there without moving.

"I know a song," Riley said. "Paul taught it to me." He giggled and started to sing:

Itsy-bitsy spider
Climbed up the kitchen door.
Along came my mom
And knocked him to the floor.
Then Riley came
With a baseball bat
And with a mighty swing
He squashed the spider flat.

Riley giggled again. "That's Paul's song. I wouldn't do that. Not really. I like spiders." Then he sang the song again.

I rolled over and looked at Riley. "You're not going back to sleep, are you?"

Riley shook his head. "It's morning. And I'm hungry."

"All right," I said. "We'll get up."

Riley bounced out of bed and ran to his dresser. He looked in the top drawer and said, "I don't have any more shirts." Then he ran to the closet and dug into that big pile. "Yes, I do." He pulled out a shirt and put it on.

"You know what I'd do if I were you?" I said.

"What, big brother?"

"I'd get those French fries out of there. If you leave food around, you can get mice or ants."

"Oooh." Riley grabbed the wastebasket and pawed through the pile. "I hate ants," he said. "It would be neat to have a mouse. But I hate ants."

While Riley was looking for fries, I lay back on my pillow. Things had to be different today. I had to make Joan like me. I wanted her to invite me to come back and visit Dad, the way I did before. And why would she invite a loser who made messes in the kitchen and then hid under the table in his underwear?

Dad was going to have a new son—Riley. And Riley was great. I didn't want Dad to forget about his old son. So I had to do better with Joan. Starting now. What I needed was a good day. No, not a good day. A perfect day.

I got dressed and went into the bathroom. I washed good and combed my hair just right. Before I finished, Riley tapped on the door. I opened it, and he poked his head in. "Hurry up, big brother. I'm so hungry I almost ate those old French fries."

We went to the kitchen. I checked the floor to be sure I hadn't missed a spot of yogurt. Riley looked into the family room. "He's here. Uncle Tony's here."

I could see somebody asleep on the folded-out couch. "Don't wake him up," I whispered.

"I won't," Riley said. "But maybe he'll wake up by himself. If he wakes up, we can watch TV."

"Be really quiet," I said.

Riley laughed. "You know what I used to do? I used to wake him up by putting a pencil up his nose. And one time I put ice on his foot. He didn't like that."

"Today we let him sleep," I said.

"Let's eat," Riley said.

"Maybe we'd better wait for your mom."

"I make my breakfast lots of times," Riley said. "I can cook stuff."

"Like what?"

"Toast. And cereal."

Those sounded pretty safe. Riley opened a cupboard and brought out boxes of bran flakes and shredded wheat. Healthy stuff. Just like at home.

"Paul has good cereal at his house," Riley said. "He has cereal with marshmallows. And he even has chocolate cereal. Mom thinks those cereals aren't good for you, but I like 'em. At Paul's house I had six bowls of chocolate cereal, and I didn't get sick. I had a little tummy ache, that's all."

I decided to have toast. Riley opened the refrigerator and got out wheat bread and fruit spread.

Hannah came into the kitchen. She was wearing a pink bathrobe and fuzzy pink slippers. She glared at Riley and me.

"Good morning," I said. It wasn't easy to smile at her, but I did it.

"You boys better not make a mess."

I moved back out of her way.

"I told you she was grumpy in the morning," Riley whispered.

Hannah took the last of the purple juice and grabbed a banana from a basket.

"That's the last banana," Riley said. "You could share."

Hannah moved around the kitchen while she ate. She handed the banana peel to Riley. "Here. Don't ever say I never gave you anything." She marched out of the room.

We heard the bathroom door close. "She'll be in there for an hour," Riley said. "She keeps doing her hair over and over."

I put two pieces of bread in the toaster. Riley poured some bran flakes into a bowl. I grabbed up two flakes that he spilled.

Riley brought the milk jug out of the refrigerator. "Let me help you with that," I said.

"I got it, big brother." But he poured the milk too fast, and it went slopping out of the bowl, taking bran flakes with it. Riley jerked his arm back and sloshed more milk on the floor.

"Oh, no," I moaned.

"I'll get the mop," Riley said. He raced through the

family room and out the far door. A minute later he came back in, carrying the mop like a baseball bat.

Tony sat up in bed and said something. Riley dropped the mop and ran over to Tony. "Hey, Tony," he yelled. "How's my main man?" They shook hands and wrestled a little. "I have a new big brother. Isn't that neat?" Riley waved me over. "Hey, Dan, come here and meet Tony."

Tony looked pretty sleepy, but he smiled at me. He had a little black mustache and a gold earring in his left ear. He held out a hand. "What do you say, Dan?"

"Hi." We shook hands the regular way. Then he gave me a high five.

"Uncle Tony," Riley said, "I wanted to stay up till you got here. But Mom said you'd be late. Did you come in late?"

"No, I got here early. Early in the morning. About two or so."

Riley bounced up and down on the bed. "How come you were so late?"

"I went to a movie with this cute girl. And I had a hard time saying good night to her."

Riley giggled. "Did you kiss her?"

"Don't get nosy," Tony said.

"I'll bet you did," Riley said. "Yuk."

48

Tony looked at me. "Things a little crazy around here?"

"Not too bad," I said.

"Joanie's a little nervous on good days. Right now I'll bet she's wound pretty tight."

BLAAAAT.

I heard the horrible noise, but I didn't know what it was. I looked over my shoulder at the kitchen and saw a cloud of black smoke.

"It's the smoke detector," Riley yelled. He sounded happy about it.

The horrible blatting sound kept coming. Riley and I ran to the kitchen, with Tony right behind us. We got there in time to see Joan come rushing in. She stepped into the milk and slipped, catching herself on the table before she fell.

Smoke was pouring out of the toaster. Tony reached around us and punched the button. Black toast popped up. Then Tony opened a window and used a magazine to fan the air by the detector. The blatting stopped.

"Nice way to wake up," Tony said to Joan.

Joan stood in the same spot, her bare foot still in the milk. "I can't believe this," she said. I was pretty sure she was looking at me.

Tony grabbed a towel and handed it to her. "We'll

49

take care of this," he said. "Riley went out to get the mop, but I started talking to him. Give us two minutes. We'll have it all cleaned up."

Joan let out a long breath but didn't say anything. She wiped off her foot, then handed the towel to Riley. She walked away, shaking her head.

So much for my perfect day.

Chapter SIX

"Look at this," Tony said. "You guys had the toaster control all the way over to dark." He used the magazine to fan the smoke away.

"I didn't touch the toaster," Riley said. Then he looked at me and said, "It's okay, big brother. It was an accident. And it didn't hurt anything."

I knew it was no accident. I had put in the bread, but I hadn't touched the control. But good old Hannah had been walking around the kitchen.

Riley and Hannah went to school. Riley begged his mom to let him stay home with Tony and me. "Please, Mom," he said. "Pretty, pretty please."

Joan shook her head. "I already said no."

"Come on," Riley said. "Ple-e-e-e-ease."

Tony grabbed Riley and carried him to the door. "Get out of here, Riley. Dan and I'll pick you up right after school."

Riley grinned. "Come early and park by the flagpole. That way we can see your truck from my room."

After Tony got dressed, I helped him fold up the couch. Then we sat around and watched cartoons. I was surprised that a college guy would watch *Roadrunner* and *Bugs Bunny*, but he sat there and laughed.

Tony didn't really look like a college guy. He wore baggy pants and a backward baseball cap and a T-shirt that said ALCATRAZ SWIM TEAM.

Dad called. Joan brought me the cordless phone. "It's your father." She gave me a nice smile. I hoped she meant it.

"Hey, buddy, how'd you sleep?" Dad asked me.

"Fine," I lied.

"Are you okay?"

"Sure."

"Listen, buddy, I'm up to my ears here. I'm really sorry. Maybe you and Tony can hang out this morning."

"That's fine," I said. Three lies in a row.

"I'll see you this afternoon at the tux shop," he said. "I was hoping we'd have some time, but—"

"I'm fine," I said. I wasn't, but I wasn't going to let anybody know that.

"Great. Let me talk to Joan again." We said goodbye, and I handed the phone to Joan. She walked back to the kitchen while she talked.

A few minutes later she was back. "How are you guys doing?"

"Fine," I said.

"This is a tough life," Tony said. "Lying around, watching cartoons."

"Tony," Joan said, "I have a favor to ask you."

Tony laughed. "It'll cost you money."

Joan didn't smile. "I'd like you not to wear your earring for the wedding."

Tony shrugged. "You think a tux and an earring don't go together? No problem. Just so I can wear my cap." Joan gave him a funny look. Tony waved his hands. "I'm joking, I'm joking."

"Thank you," Joan said, and walked away.

Once she was gone, Tony turned to me. "She wants this wedding to be perfect. She's kind of scared. You see, our mom and dad got divorced. And we hated it. She said it would never happen to her. And it did. This time she wants everything perfect. Starting with the wedding."

I didn't say anything. I just hoped I didn't mess things up somehow.

A woman rang the doorbell. She and Joan sat down at the kitchen table and started looking through papers. "Tony, could you turn that down?" Joan called. "I can't think with that noise going on."

Tony clicked off the TV. "We're on our way out. Dan and I have things to do."

"Don't forget that you're picking up Riley," Joan said. "He gets out at one forty-five. And you're all meeting at the tux shop at two."

"We can handle that," Tony said, heading for the door.

"What about lunch?" Joan called after us.

"We'll get something downtown," Tony said. "Something good and greasy."

Joan waved us away. "Don't forget about Riley."

Tony closed the door, and we walked down the driveway. "I'm glad to get out of there," he said. "She's going crazy right now."

"Do you really have some things to do?" I asked.

Tony laughed. "Sure. Important things. Like driving around. And chasing girls." He pointed ahead of us. "What do you think of my machine?"

Sitting at the curb was an old white bread truck. If you looked close, you could see red letters and a loaf of bread showing through the white paint. "That's yours?"

"Don't laugh," he said. "That's a good machine. I can haul my surfboard or anything I want. If I get sleepy, I can pull over and sleep in the back. And it's so ugly, nobody would ever steal it."

The truck squeaked and rattled, but I liked riding in it. "I don't have enough gas to get to the beach," Tony said. "So we'll go to the mall."

The mall sounded better to me anyway.

Tony talked about the stereo he wanted to get for the truck. Then he looked at me and said, "This whole wedding business—things have to be funny for you right now."

"I'm doing fine."

"Hey, you don't have to talk about it. That's okay. I remember when my mom and dad got divorced. I was really mad. We had to move and everything. And my dad went off to Florida, and I never saw him. I know, man. Divorce stinks."

"I see my dad a lot," I said.

"The divorce was bad enough," Tony said. "But then my mom got married again. To old Steve. That was the worst. He can't stand to be in the same room with me. That's why I lived at Joan's about half the time. So I know how things are for you."

"It's not like that," I said. "I'm okay."

"That's cool," Tony said. "You don't have to talk about it. Let's go have some fun."

We walked through the mall so that Tony could look at the girls working in the stores. Then we went to a place called Wild World that was full of video games. I tried the race car, then a fighter-pilot machine.

A guy wearing a cowboy hat came up to us. "Sorry, kid. You can't be in here during school hours."

"Give him a break," Tony said. "The poor guy's in town for his dad's wedding. You know how rotten that is? And he has to wear a tux and all that good stuff. And act like he's all happy. Now you tell him he can't even have a little fun."

The man smiled and shook his head. "All right, he can stay." He used a key to open the front of a football machine. "Try this one next, kid. It's a good one. I'll put a couple of free games on it for you."

Later we ate cheeseburgers at a little place in the mall. "The food's not great here," Tony said. "But we get to watch Valerie." Valerie was kind of pretty, I guess. But I ended up watching her three-inch-long purple fingernails. I don't know how she kept from stabbing herself.

"You know what I'm gonna do tomorrow?" Tony said. "I'm gonna come in here wearing my tux. Valerie will love that. Girls are crazy about tuxes. Wait'll they see *you* in a tux. They'll be chasing you all over the place."

"They better not."

Tony laughed. "Don't give me that. I know about guys like you. You say you don't like girls. But there's one girl at your school that you think is special. But you keep it a big secret."

I thought about Amy Wall for a minute. I wondered how Tony knew about her.

While we sat in front of Riley's school, Tony started in about divorce again. "Look," I said, "I'm fine. I'm not mad about anything. I'm glad Dad's happy. Everything's fine."

"And you never wished your mom and dad would get back together? Not even once?"

"Maybe. I mean, it'd be nice to have Dad around all the time. But I'm not mad."

Tony punched my arm. "That's okay. You don't have to talk about it."

Riley was excited about riding in the bread truck. He had Tony drive around the block once so everybody could see us. "Could I wear your cap, Uncle Tony?" he asked.

Riley put the cap on backward. It was way too big, but he used one hand to hold it on. Then he leaned out the window, calling to his buddies and waving the other hand like crazy.

Dad wasn't at the tux shop when we got there. But the woman at the shop wanted us to try everything on. She told Riley and me what to put on first and how to do the buttons. Then I went into one of the little rooms and got dressed. There were even special shiny shoes for me to wear.

"You look marvelous," she told me when I came out.

I kept looking at myself in the mirror when nobody was watching. I looked different. But I couldn't decide whether I looked great or stupid.

"Oh, man," Tony said, "we are one fine-looking bunch."

Riley looked in the mirror and giggled. "I don't look like me."

After we put on our regular clothes again, the woman folded the tuxes and put them back into plastic bags. Then we stood around and waited for Dad. Riley told Tony all the dumb jokes I had heard the night before.

Dad came rushing in. The woman wanted him to try on his tux, but he said he didn't have time. He paid the bill while Tony and I put the tuxes in the trunk of Dad's car.

"I get to ride in Tony's truck," Riley said.

"Dan," Dad said to me, "why don't you ride with me?"

"We'll race you," Riley said.

As soon as we got in the car, Dad said, "How are you doing?"

I thought about the burned toast and hiding under the table in my underwear. And I wondered how often I'd be seeing Dad now. But I just said, "Okay."

"I'm sorry things are so crazy right now," Dad said. "I'm taking time off after the wedding, so I have to take care of everything at the office now. I was hoping we'd get some time together. But things keep going wrong."

"It's okay."

"Did you and Tony have some fun?"

I told him about the video games. "Those things are great," he said. "But they gobble up your money. Are you broke?"

"I have some money left."

Dad took out his wallet and gave me a twenty-dollar bill. "You may need to buy something before you get home."

We stopped in front of Hannah's school. Hannah came running over to the car with another girl.

Dad rolled down the window and said, "Hi there."

"I want you to meet Lisa," Hannah said. "Lisa, this is my new dad."

Dad and Lisa said hi. Then Dad said, "And this is Dan."

Lisa looked over at me for half a second and said hi. I said hello, but nobody was listening. Hannah was going on about the wedding.

Finally Dad said, "We'd better go, Hannah. Your mom's taking you to the hairdresser."

Hannah still didn't get into the car. "Can I ride in front?" she asked Dad. "I have something to show you."

Dad looked over at me. "Hey, Dan's already there. Hop in the back."

Hannah gave me this special look. Like she'd just found something in the back of the refrigerator that was covered with blue mold. Then she smiled at Dad and got into the backseat.

Hannah put on her seat belt, but it must have been very loose. At every red light she leaned forward and hung over Dad's shoulder. She had a drawing she'd done in art class.

I didn't get a good look at it. She was holding it so only Dad could see it. Like it was some big secret.

"I did what you said," she told him. "I quit worrying and did the best I could. And it was kind of fun."

"That's great," Dad said. "I like it."

"I still don't like art," she said, "but I don't hate it."

"The light's green," I said, just before the cars behind us starting blasting their horns.

At the next light Hannah was back with her picture, pointing at little stuff. "See the rainbow? Oh, look, the man only has one shoe. I'll fix that." She sat back and got out a felt-tip pen.

Dad turned down a quiet street. A big rubber ball came bouncing out in front of us. Dad slammed on the brakes, and we all got jerked forward. Hannah's hand came flying up and smacked me by the ear.

"Sorry," Dad said. "I saw that ball, and I was afraid a kid would be running after it."

"Oh, look what I did," Hannah said, laughing.

It took me a second to catch on. She had hit me with her pen, putting a black streak on my ear, down my neck, and onto my shirt. "Real funny," I said.

"It was my fault," Dad said.

"Well, I didn't mean to," Hannah said.

"Of course you didn't," Dad told her. And Hannah gave me one of her special looks.

When we got to Joan's house, Dad sent Hannah into the house. "Your mom's waiting for you."

"Thank you for the ride," Hannah said, reaching over the seat and giving him a hug.

While she ran up the driveway, Dad said, "Take it easy, Dan. It was an accident."

I knew better than to argue with him. "I don't have any more shirts," I said.

"It's okay, buddy. That ink will come off."

I looked over at him. "Dad, she hates me."

Dad shook his head. "She doesn't hate you. How could anybody hate a guy like you?"

"She acts like it."

Dad smiled. "Give her a little time. You guys will get used to each other." He laughed and tapped my shoulder. "Hey, things are going to be fine."

I didn't believe that for a minute. But I didn't say so.

I looked down at my watch. My plane for San Francisco would be leaving in twenty-seven hours.

Chapter SEVEN

Dad rushed off to do something, and I spent the afternoon with Tony and Riley. We threw the Frisbee for a while, then played video games in the family room. We ended up watching cartoons again.

"Uncle Tony," Riley said, "remember when we used to play bucking bronco?"

Tony laughed. "Sure. You used to wear me out."

"Could we do it once more? Please."

"You were a lot littler then," Tony said. "I don't think I can hold you now."

"Please," Riley said. "I want to show Dan."

"Don't give me that," Tony said. "You just want a ride."

Riley laughed. "But Dan wants to see me ride, don't you, Dan?"

"I guess," I said.

Tony got down on his hands and knees. "No kicking. One kick, and the old horse quits."

Riley climbed onto Tony's back. "Come on, horsie."

"Hold on tight," Tony said. "The old bucking bronco is feeling wild."

Tony bounced up and down a few times, and Riley started yelling, "Go, go, go!" Tony spun one way, then the other. Riley grabbed Tony's shirt with both hands and managed to hang on.

Then Tony bounced two times, and Riley went flying off to the side. He banged into a little table, and a lamp came crashing down. I heard glass break.

"Be careful," Tony said. "Don't cut yourself."

"Mom's gonna be mad," Riley said.

Tony, still on his hands and knees, moved toward the lamp. "No problem. It's just the bulb. I'll get a broom. Do you know where the dustpan is?"

"I think so," Riley said. He and Tony went out the door. I stayed on the couch so that I wouldn't get into the glass, but I reached over and picked up the lamp. The white shade had a big dent in it. I unscrewed the little thing that held on the shade.

Right then Joan and Hannah walked in. Joan took one look at me and said, "What are you doing?"

"Look at the glass," Hannah said.

There I was, lying on the couch, with a broken lamp and a dented shade. And glass all over the floor.

I couldn't think of a thing to say.

Tony and Riley came rushing in. "No problem, Sis," Tony said. "We just had a little accident. We'll get it cleaned up in no time."

"Nice going, guys," Hannah said. She went off to her room.

Joan shook her head. I knew she wanted to scream. But her voice came out quiet. Too quiet. "We have to get dressed and be out of here by six o'clock. That gives us ten minutes."

"Tony and Dan didn't do it," Riley yelled. "I did it."

Joan turned away from us. "Take care of it," she said. "And get dressed."

Tony laughed as soon as she was gone. "Man, I thought she was gonna explode."

Tony swept up the glass while Riley and I ran to his room. I put on my itchy blue suit and hurried back to help Tony. By then, he was in the bathroom. He came out wearing slacks and a blue shirt. The baseball cap was gone, but he was still wearing the earring. "Killer suit," he told me. "You'll have the girls chasing you all over the place."

Tony helped Riley put on a necktie. "Where's your tie, Uncle Tony?" Riley asked.

"I have to wear one tomorrow with the tux," Tony said. "That's enough for me."

Riley looked at the kitchen clock. "It's one minute after six. So we're late. You think I should tell Mom?"

Tony laughed. "Sure. If you want to get killed."

I didn't know what to expect at a wedding rehearsal. Mostly it was just people standing around. Joan and Dad talked to some woman, and the three of them walked around the church.

Riley and I sat on a wooden bench with Tony. Some people came over to say hello, and Tony told me their names. I forgot them right away.

I met Riley's grandmother. "You've got your daddy's good looks," she said to me.

"It's the suit," Tony said after she left. "Women love it."

Riley grabbed me. "See that old lady that just came in? Watch out for her. That's Aunt Bertha. She kisses everybody."

"This is a bummer," Tony said. "Here I am all dressed up, and the only girls my age are my cousins."

"What's your job in the wedding?" I asked him.

"My part's easy. I walk in with Joanie, then sit down. It's what my dad would do if he was here. But he's not here."

I started to ask about that, but I let it go.

When Joan and Dad came by us, Riley called out, "Mom, can we go outside?"

"Stay right there," Joan said. "And don't get into anything."

I was pretty sure she meant that for me.

When we finally got started, I saw that the wedding would be like the last one I went to—with kids in the middle of things. The kind of wedding I had called stupid last night, right in front of Joan and Dad.

I was best man, which meant I stood in front, next to Dad. Hannah was maid of honor. She marched in and stood next to Joan. Riley was the ringbearer. He marched in with the rings, then stood next to me. So once the service got going, the five of us were up there in front of the preacher. And, sure enough, Dad and Joan had special things to say about how they'd work together to raise the kids and be one family. I felt really dumb—again.

When the rehearsal was finally over, I rode to the restaurant in Tony's truck. "You okay?" he asked me.

"I'm fine," I said.

"It's okay, man. You don't have to talk about it."

The restaurant was called The Islander. There were

canoes on the wall and lots of palm trees. Riley came running up to Tony and me. "It stinks in here," he said. "Like fish."

We had a special room in the back, set up for about thirty people. There was one long table and some other regular tables. Riley said he and I had to sit at the long table. "That's the head table," Tony said. "You guys are the stars."

A woman with flowers in her hair gave us red punch. Our glasses had little umbrellas in them. I emptied my glass right away. This time I wasn't going to spill anything.

"Listen," Tony told me, "you'll have to give a little speech after dinner."

"No way," I said.

"I mean it. That's what they do."

"I can't give a speech."

"No problem," he said. "Just say you're happy to be part of this whole mess."

"I want to do it right," I said. "Tell me what to say."

"Keep it simple. Say, 'I'm happy to be part of this celebration.' Then you raise your glass and say, 'Here's to many years of happiness.' How's that?"

I had him say it over and over until I got every word right.

The dinner was terrible. I was put at one end of the head table, with Joan next to me. I tried to do everything right, but it wasn't easy. The salad tasted like fish with stinky cheese. Then we did have fish—covered with some brown goo. For dessert we had bowls of fruit. The only thing I recognized was pineapple. And that was also the only thing that tasted good.

I kept waiting for the speeches, hoping I wouldn't forget mine. Dad got up and thanked everybody for coming. He talked about how happy he was and how lucky. Everybody clapped. Joan said the same thing—in a speech that wasn't much longer than mine. Then Hannah got up and went on and on about how glad she was to have a new dad. She told about all the things she and Dad had done and how much fun he was.

The whole thing bothered me. Dad had already taken her to most of the places he'd taken me. And to places I'd never been. And now she was going to have him right there in her house.

When Hannah hugged Dad and sat down, I knew I was next. Dad stood up and said, "My son Dan would like to say a word or two."

That was as big a lie as he ever told in his life.

My mouth was too dry for me to talk. I grabbed my glass and took two big gulps of water. But a piece of ice came with the water. It was too big to swallow, and I couldn't spit it out with everybody looking at me.

While I stood up, I used my tongue to push the ice into my cheek. I looked out and saw Tony. He gave me a thumbs-up signal.

"I'm glad to be part of this—" Just then I thought of Tony's word—"mess." But I managed to get "celebration" out of my mouth. I was almost done. I raised my water glass. "Here's to many years of happy mess."

I didn't mean to say that, of course. It just slipped out. Then I didn't know what to do. So I sat down and hoped nobody would notice. People clapped like nothing was wrong, and I felt a little better.

But as soon as we were finished, Hannah came rushing over. "I can't believe it," she told me. "You know what you said? You said, 'Many years of happy mess.'"

I glanced at my watch. My plane would be leaving in twenty-two hours.

Chapter EIGHT

Riley and I rode back to the house with Joan. Tony went off in his truck. "I think I'll go say hi to Valerie," he told me.

Joan sent Riley and me off to his room. "Let me tell you good night now," she said. "You boys don't have to go to bed right away, but don't stay up too late. Tomorrow's a big day." She kissed Riley, then smiled at me and said, "Good night, Dan."

Some women were coming over to work on Joan's dress. They didn't want Riley and me around. That didn't bother us. We didn't want to be there.

The only problem was that we were starving. Riley hadn't eaten any more of his dinner than I had. "What did you hate worst?" he asked me.

"The salad, I guess."

"You know what was in mine? A little fish. And it still had bones in it." Riley held his nose. "And that rotten gravy on that rotten fish—that was sick. But your dad was neat. He gave me his roll and an extra one. So I had three rolls."

"I think the extra one was mine," I said. "I didn't even know we had rolls."

Riley got Melvin out of his cage. Melvin went walking up Riley's bare arm. I moved back a few feet. That spider still gave me the creeps. "You know what Tony and I did once?" Riley said.

"What?"

"Promise not to tell?" He went on before I could answer. "We went out and got pizza. We sneaked out the window and went down to the park. There's a phone there. We ordered a pizza and ate it right there on the picnic table."

"They delivered it to the park?"

"Tony gave them the address of a house across the street. Then when the pizza guy came, Tony caught him before he went to the house. It was neat."

I knew better. It was late, and we were supposed to be in bed. But I was starving. And the more I thought about pizza, the hungrier I got.

"How long does it take?" I asked.

"Not very long," Riley said. "You want to do it?"

"What about you?"

"I want to. But I don't have much money."

"Dad gave me twenty dollars today," I said.

Riley smiled. "What kind do you like?"

I looked at Riley. Right then was the time to stop. And I knew it. But I said, "Pepperoni."

Riley laughed and put Melvin back in his cage. "Me too, big brother."

We locked the bedroom door. Then we put a chair under the window so we could climb out easier. Riley got up on the sill, and I helped him get turned around so that he could drop down. I hurried after him.

We sneaked away from the house, staying in the shadows. We could hear women talking inside, but all the curtains were pulled.

It was farther to the park than I thought. We walked five or six blocks before we came to a big street that had too many cars on it.

"Do we have to go down this street?" I asked Riley. I was afraid some friend of Joan's might see us.

"That's how you get to the park," he said. "Let's go."

I had a bad feeling right then. It was around ten o'clock. Too late for a little guy like Riley to be hanging out.

There was a high brick wall right next to the sidewalk. I stayed close to that wall, hoping nobody would notice us. Every time a car drove past, I held my breath.

"You see where those lights are?" Riley said. "That's the park." The lights were at least two blocks ahead.

Another car drove past us, heading the other way. But this one had red and blue lights on top. I saw the sign on the door. "Police," I whispered.

The brake lights of the police car flashed. I knew we'd been spotted.

"Quick," I said. "Over the wall."

"I don't know if I can make it," Riley said.

I grabbed him and pushed him up the wall. He scooted up and disappeared over the top. I glanced over my shoulder and saw the police car making a U-turn. I clawed my way up the wall and went diving over.

I landed with a thud on hard dirt. "You okay?" Riley asked.

I jumped up. "Let's get out of here."

We were in somebody's backyard. The house was dark, except for one window. I ran toward the dark side of the house. Riley was right behind me.

I heard a car stop on the other side of the wall. I kept running, right past the house to a sidewalk in front. Riley and I ran along the sidewalk until we got to a corner. We turned right and ran some more.

At the next corner we slowed to a walk. "Oh, man," Riley said, "the cops were after us."

"We're okay now," I said.

"You think they'd put us in jail?"

"No. But they'd probably take us back to your place. Your mom wouldn't be too happy about that."

We walked for a long time. None of the streets were straight, and it was hard to figure out directions. I kept thinking we'd come to a regular street pretty soon. But it didn't happen.

At the next corner I checked the street signs. We were at the corner of Something Circle and Something Court. I knew that a court was a dead end, so we stayed with the circle. But we kept running into other courts and other circles.

"I'm getting tired," Riley said. "Real tired."

"Sit down and rest for a second."

Riley plopped down on the sidewalk. "Are we lost?"

"We'll be okay."

I gave Riley a few minutes, then pulled him to his feet. "Time to get rolling."

We walked another block. Then Riley pulled on my arm. "I have to tell you something. I don't want you to get mad."

"I won't get mad."

"Promise?"

"What is it?"

"I never went to get pizza before. Tony and his buddies did. And he told me about it. But I never did it."

"Oh, man," I said, "you lied to me."

"You promised you wouldn't get mad."

"Maybe I lied to *you*. Serves you right."

We didn't say anything for a block or two. Then Riley asked, "Are you still mad?"

"I'm just tired. And sick of this stupid place. I think we're going in circles."

"Can we stop and rest again?" Riley asked. "I can't go any farther." He sat down on the curb. "I think I'm getting a blister."

"Just a little more," I said. "If we don't get to a real street, I'll go up and ask somebody."

"Couldn't you do it now?"

After the rest, Riley walked even slower. And all the houses and all the streets looked the same. I had to get some help.

I waited until I saw a house with plenty of lights on. Then I went up and rang the doorbell. Riley stayed about ten feet back.

An old man on crutches opened the door a few inches and looked at me.

"Could you help me?" I asked. "We're lost. We can't find our way out of here."

The man looked at me, then looked over my shoulder at Riley. "What are you boys doing out this time of night?"

"Taking a walk," I said.

"We were going to get pizza," Riley said.

"Wait here a second." The man moved away from the door, then came back with a phone. He handed it to me.

"I don't need a phone," I said. "I just want to know how to get out of here. We keep going in circles."

"You'd better call your mom and dad," the man said.

Riley sank down onto the steps. "Yeah," he said.

I didn't want to make that call. And I knew I didn't have to. We could just walk away. An old man on crutches couldn't chase us. Sooner or later we'd find our way home.

But then I looked at Riley. He was sitting on a step, bent over, his head resting on his knees. He was finished.

I took out my wallet and found Dad's cell-phone number. I punched the buttons, hoping Dad was carrying that phone. I hated to think of calling Joan.

When Dad said hello, I told him it was me. "What's going on?" he asked.

I had to think for a minute. It was hard to explain what had happened. "Dad," I said finally, "I did something dumb. Again."

The man gave Dad directions to his house. He stayed on the porch with Riley and me until Dad came.

When Riley saw Dad's car, he got up and ran toward it. "Don't get mad at Dan," he told Dad. "It was my idea."

"It was my fault," I called. "I knew better."

Dad got out of the car and looked at us. "You know what I think? I think you're both beanbrains. Running around out here in the middle of the night. That's really stupid."

"I'm sorry," I said.

"I'm sorry too," Riley said.

"Then that makes three of us," Dad said. "This is *not* what we need tonight."

Dad thanked the man, and we drove back toward Riley's house. We went on a whole bunch of circles before we got back to regular streets. "I can see how you got lost," Dad said.

Riley's house was dark. Dad parked at the curb and

looked at us. "You guys came out the bedroom window?"

"Yeah," I said.

"I don't know what to do here," Dad said. "I hate to wake Joan right now." He turned and looked at us. "Have you guys learned anything?"

"Yes," we both said.

"Is this going to happen again?"

"No," we both said.

"All right. Go back in the window. And you better be quiet."

I looked over at Dad. "Thanks, Dad," I said. "I mean it. Thanks a lot." But then I didn't want him to leave. "Can you wait just a minute? I'll help Riley get inside. Then I want to ask you something."

I lifted Riley up so he could climb in the window. "I'll be there in two minutes," I told him.

"I'll be asleep by then," he said. "I think maybe I'm asleep right now."

I hurried back to the car and got in. I pulled the door shut without slamming it. "I'm sorry," I said. "It was really dumb."

"Yeah," Dad said. "But it's over now."

"Yeah." I wanted to say something else, but I

couldn't think how to say it. I ended up just sitting there.

Finally Dad asked, "Are you okay?"

"I guess." But then I went on. "Joan thinks I'm a loser. When I'm around her, nothing goes right."

"That's not true."

"Yes, it is. You weren't there. I keep doing dumb stuff. And what I want to know is, what if she hates me?"

"She doesn't hate you."

"But what if she does? Will you still come and see me?"

Dad laughed. "Don't be silly. Of course I'll come and see you. Nothing has changed with you and me."

That made me mad. "That's a big lie," I shouted. "And you know it. Everything's changed. You're getting married, and you have two new kids. And you're gonna be living right in the house with them. And I'm gonna be clear up in San Francisco." I was crying by then. I don't know when I started. "I hate it. I hate the whole thing—the wedding, everything."

"It's okay to feel that way." Dad reached out and squeezed my shoulder. "But I think you'll change your mind. Hey, you've got a new buddy with Riley. He thinks you're great."

"Riley's fine," I said. "But then there's Hannah."

"Give her a little time," Dad said.

"Maybe a hundred years."

Dad laughed. "We'll see. I think things will get better. But sometimes you have to take the bad with the good. I'm really happy to be marrying Joan. But do you think I want to live in the same house with a tarantula?"

"But that's—" I started.

"Listen," Dad said, "some things don't change. I'll always want to see you. And I will. No matter what else happens, you and I are still the same. You believe that?"

"I guess."

"Things are a little rocky now. And we're all pretty tired. But everything's going to work out. Just wait and see, okay?"

"Okay."

He squeezed my shoulder again and laughed. "Hey, I know what you need right now. You need some of my health food."

"What?"

"Best medicine around. Look in the glove box."

I opened it and found two candy bars. "These are health food?"

"Don't laugh. They're my secret formula. Your mother and Joan don't understand, but sometimes there's no medicine like good old chocolate."

I laughed. "Come on, Dad."

"I'm serious," Dad said, but he was laughing too. "Try one. See if it helps."

I did. And it did.

Chapter NINE

Riley and I spent most of the morning with Tony. "Our job," Tony told us, "is to stay out of the way."

We sat on the floor in Riley's room, and Tony taught us to play blackjack. Riley had trouble adding his points, but he still won most of the time. So did I. I think Tony may have been sneaking us good cards. "You guys are too lucky," he told us. "If we were playing for money, you'd own my truck by now."

At eleven o'clock we went to the mall and got hamburgers. Riley and I wanted pizza, but Tony said no. "You don't want to be stinking up the wedding with your pepperoni breath."

We even stopped at Wild World and played video games.

"This is great," Riley said. "I just wish we didn't have to go to the wedding."

The wedding was at two o'clock. But Tony got Riley and me to the church, dressed in our tuxes, by a little after one. We even beat Dad there.

My tux felt tight all over. Wearing it was like being

tied up. But Tony said I looked great. "You're gonna need a club to fight off the girls."

"Yuk," Riley said.

"Be real careful," Tony said before we got out of the truck. "You guys look fantastic, and you don't want to get messed up. Don't lean against anything. And be careful where you sit."

"Is it okay to breathe?" I asked.

Tony laughed. He looked in the mirror and fooled with his hair. "Oh, man, sometimes I wish I was rich instead of handsome."

"Are you gonna wear your earring?" Riley asked him. "Mom said you weren't."

Tony smiled and looked in the mirror again. "I won't take it out till the last minute. It'll give your mom something to fuss about."

Riley looked at me. "Mom says I can't get an earring until I'm twenty-one."

"They've got earrings that clip on," Tony said. "Someday I'll get one for you, and we'll come in and show your mom."

"When?" Riley asked. "When?"

"Not today," Tony said. "Today we'll go easy on her. Everything's gonna be perfect." He opened his door.

"Watch where you walk. You don't want to get gum or dog doo on those fancy shoes."

I left my suitcase in Tony's truck. He was taking me to the airport after the reception.

When Dad came into the church, he looked different. It wasn't just the tux. He looked kind of scared. He took Riley and me to a little room in the back. He had us sit down, but he kept walking back and forth.

I had been feeling funny before. Watching Dad walk up and down made me feel worse. I wanted him to say something. Maybe tell one of his dumb jokes. Anything. Finally I said, "Dad, are you okay?"

He smiled. "Sure. A little nervous, I guess."

Riley's mouth dropped open. "You're not gonna run away, are you?"

Dad laughed. "No. What makes you ask that?"

"I saw this movie," Riley said. "And the guy got scared and ran off right before the wedding."

"I'm here for good," Dad said.

Riley ran over and gave Dad a bear hug. "Good."

Watching them bothered me. I felt left out. Like Dickie Moore, that kid who always gets picked last.

But Dad looked over at me and said, "Yeah, I'm

here for good. And so is Dan. We're all together from now on."

Riley let go of Dad and gave me a high five. "Me and you, big brother."

"Right," I said.

Dad kept walking up and down after that, but I felt better.

Just before two o'clock, Tony came to get Riley. "I'll be right there," Riley said. He took me over to a corner. "I got something for you. It's a present." He handed me a little white box. There was no ribbon on it, and the box wasn't even new. It had holes in the top.

"What is it?" I asked.

"It's a surprise," he said. "Don't open it until you're on the plane."

"Thanks, Riley." I figured it was something to eat—a candy bar, maybe, or a pack of gum. That was fine with me.

My coat didn't have any pockets, so I put the box into a front pocket of my pants. It made a bulge, but the bottom of my coat covered it.

The wedding started late, but Dad said weddings were always like that. Dad and I came in the side door and stood up in front.

"It's crazy," Dad whispered. "As soon as I get out

here in front of everybody, all these places start itching. Maybe we could sneak out for a quick scratch."

We waited a long time before the organ began to play. Riley marched in first, carrying the rings on a blue pillow. He looked great in his tux. And he walked really slow, taking little steps, exactly the way they'd told him to.

Then Hannah came in with a big smile. She looked like she'd never done a rotten thing in her whole life.

Everybody stood up when Joan and Tony came in, both with giant smiles. Joan was wearing a long yellow dress that touched the floor. Tony had taken out his earring. He looked like he'd been wearing tuxes all his life.

Everything went perfect. Dad and Joan made all their promises. The preacher said all his things. Then right after Dad and Joan said the "for richer, for poorer" stuff, it was time for the rings. That was my one job.

I was supposed to get the rings off Riley's pillow and hand them to the preacher. The rings were pinned to the pillow so they wouldn't get lost. I was to unpin them and put them in my right hand, then walk over and hand them to the preacher.

There was no way I was going to mess up. I unfastened the safety pin and set both rings on the palm of my right hand. I walked over and held them out to the preacher, and he took them out of my hand.

I moved back to my standing place—half a step back from Dad. I felt great. I hadn't messed up. No dropped rings. No fumbling around.

The preacher held up the rings and said a prayer. While he was talking, I heard Hannah make a funny noise. I looked over at her. Her face was twisted up, like she was about to scream.

Hannah saw me looking at her. Keeping her hands in front of her so that nobody behind us could see, she pointed toward Joan.

I saw it right away. A tarantula. It was crawling up the skirt of Joan's yellow dress. It had to be Melvin. There couldn't be two spiders that big.

The tarantula was on the right side of Joan's skirt, the side brushing against Dad. I started to move, but Hannah held up her hand. She mouthed "Wait," without making a sound.

I looked back at Riley. He wasn't even looking my way. He was fooling with the safety pin on the pillow. Besides, he was too far away. I'd have to do this one by myself.

Dad put the ring on Joan's finger, and he repeated

the words the preacher said. Much too slowly. Melvin was still moving higher. Almost to Joan's waist.

Suddenly I realized what had happened. Riley had given me a present. Melvin. Dad was moving into their house, and Riley knew Dad hated tarantulas. So why not give Melvin to me?

And in my pants pocket there was now an empty white box. One with holes in the top.

So I was doing it again—making a mess of things. What would Joan think of me after I wrecked her wedding?

I had to do something. I took a small sideways step, but Hannah hissed. So quietly that I was probably the only one who heard her. She shook her head half an inch and mouthed "Wait" again.

Joan put a ring on Dad's finger, and she said the same words Dad had said. She couldn't have gone any slower.

The only one in a hurry was Melvin. He was on Joan's belt, then above it.

I looked over at Hannah. She still had her hand up, telling me to wait. But I didn't think she could see Melvin any longer. He was moving faster now, scooting up the side of Joan's dress.

I didn't think anybody behind us could see him

either. Dad and Joan could have seen him, of course. But they were looking into each other's eyes. And the preacher was reading from his book. But Melvin kept crawling higher.

I didn't hear any of the preacher's words until he said "husband and wife." I knew we were almost finished. But I didn't know if I could wait any longer.

Then the preacher said, "You may now kiss the bride."

When Dad put his arm around Joan, he just missed Melvin. Melvin went scooting up to Joan's shoulder.

That was it. While Dad kissed Joan, I stepped close and grabbed Melvin in my bare hand.

Joan turned toward me with a surprised look on her face. I still had my hand almost on her shoulder. Then she smiled and said, "How nice." She bent down and kissed me right on the lips.

Hannah grabbed Dad and kissed him, and people clapped. Then the music started, and Dad and Joan walked down the aisle together.

I couldn't close my hand around Melvin. He was too big, and I didn't want to squeeze him. So I held my cupped hand against my coat. I could feel him squiggling around in there.

Hannah and I waited, just the way we were told,

until Dad and Joan were at the tenth row. Then Hannah put her hand on my arm, and we started down the aisle.

"Oh, thank you, thank you," Hannah whispered.

I didn't say anything. I was trying to walk as smoothly as I could. I still had a live tarantula in my bare hand.

Chapter TEN

Lots of good things happened that day, and one of the big ones was this: Melvin didn't bite me. As soon as Hannah and I were outside the church, I grabbed the box out of my pocket and eased Melvin into it. Once he was in there, I slapped on the lid.

I put the box in my pocket and kept my hand clamped over it. I didn't let go of the box until I got to Tony's truck. Then I took a green shoelace from my other shoes and tied the box shut. With triple knots.

The wedding reception was better than I expected. There was lots of good food. Not all healthy stuff. There was too much kissing, but people left me alone. All except Aunt Bertha. She cried and kissed everybody. She got Riley three times.

Hannah waited until Riley went back for more food, then came over to me. "Dan," she said, "that was Riley's spider, wasn't it?"

I wasn't expecting that, but I managed to say, "No way."

"Really?" She sounded like she didn't believe me.

"Didn't you see that thing? It was twice as big as that little spider Riley had. Big old hairy legs." I hoped I wasn't overdoing it.

But Hannah nodded her head. "He *was* huge, wasn't he?"

"King Kong of the spiders," I said.

"He was so gross. I thought I was going to be sick right there in front of everybody. And you grabbed him with your bare hand. I don't know how you did that."

"I don't ever want to do it again," I said. "I kept thinking he was gonna bite me any second." I looked over at her. "You didn't really think Riley brought old Melvin to the wedding, did you? He wouldn't do that."

"You don't know Riley the way I do," she said.

"Maybe," I said. "But he doesn't even have Melvin anymore. He gave him away to some kid." That part came out easy. Maybe because it wasn't really a lie.

Hannah sighed. "It's like something out of a bad dream." Then she stopped. "Did you tell Riley about the spider?"

"I didn't tell anybody."

"Good. Don't. Especially not Riley. He can't keep a secret even if he wants to. You'll find that out when you've been around a while."

So Hannah figured I'd be around a while. I liked that. "I won't tell him."

"Don't tell anybody. Please. The whole wedding was perfect. And Mom's really, really happy. It would wreck everything if she found out a tarantula had been crawling on her."

"I know what you mean," I said.

Hannah smiled. "So it's our secret. Deal?" She held out her hand.

"Deal." I held out my hand. "You sure you want to shake my hand? It might still have tarantula hair on it."

She laughed, and we shook hands.

I felt better after that. Hannah and I might not be best pals, but I could get along with her.

Riley came back with another plate of food, mostly potato chips. "I saw you shake hands with Hannah."

"We decided to be friends," I told him.

Riley thought about that for a minute. "But you and me—we're better friends, right?"

"Right," I said.

He giggled. "Wait till you open your present. You're gonna be surprised."

Just before Dad and Joan left, she came over to me. "Dan," she said, "we haven't had much chance to talk.

I'll do better next time. I promise. But I didn't want to leave without telling you something. This has been a perfect day. Absolutely perfect. And one of the nicest memories I'll have from this day is when you reached out to kiss me. That meant a lot."

I couldn't think of anything to say. Again. But that time it didn't matter. She hugged me anyway.

Tony took me to the airport. Riley wanted to come along, but he and Hannah had to go somewhere with their grandmother. I had changed my clothes, but Tony was still wearing his tux. "It may be a long time before I wear one of these things again," he said. "I'm gonna make the most of it." He reached into the back and grabbed his cap. He put it on, backward as usual. "But I can do it my way."

"Tony," I said, "I need to stop at a park or something. Somewhere with lots of trees and bushes."

"Why? You have to go to the bathroom?"

I thought about making up a story. But I had already gotten away with one bunch of lies that day. That was plenty. So I told Tony all about Melvin. He laughed and laughed. "Oh, man, Joan would have died."

"Don't tell anybody, all right?"

"Okay, for now. But that story's too good not to tell. We'll wait five years. No, ten. When your dad and Joan have their tenth anniversary, we'll tell 'em."

"All right." That was soon enough for me.

"So now you want to let Melvin go?"

"My mom would kill me if I brought him home. And I don't want him anyway. I don't know what I'll tell Riley."

"Tell him your mom wouldn't let you keep him."

"That's no lie," I said.

"I'll tell you a secret," Tony said. "Riley tried to give him to me yesterday. He wanted to get Melvin out of the house before your dad moved in."

"And you didn't want him?"

"Come on. What would I do with a stupid tarantula?" He laughed. "So Riley wasn't taking any chances with you. He told you not to open the box until you were on the plane. By then, it'd be too late to give him back."

Tony drove to a place where there weren't any houses close by. "Lots of brush and trees here," he said. "This is as good as any."

I got out of the car and set the box under a bush. I untied the shoelace, then lifted off the top. I jumped back and hopped in the truck.

We drove for a mile or two before I said, "What do you think's gonna happen to him?"

"Melvin? Oh, he'll be fine. Lots of bugs for him to eat around here. And, who knows? Maybe tomorrow some kid'll find him and take him home. And his dad will be in the movies, and the dad will take one look at Melvin and decide Melvin's got the right look. And so Melvin will end up being a movie star—Marvelous Melvin."

I laughed. "That's neat."

"Hey, why stop there? Maybe tonight another movie guy will see me in this tux, and he'll say, 'That boy can be a star!' And pretty soon you'll go to the movies and see me and Marvelous Melvin in a great movie, *Tony and the Tarantula*. And I'll be rich and famous, driving around in a limo."

"Don't get rid of your truck," I said. "Give it to me."

"Why not?" Tony said. "If I get to be a movie star, you can have my truck."

I liked that idea. I could picture myself zipping across the Golden Gate Bridge in my old white truck.

Of course, I didn't really expect Tony to become a movie star. But you never know. I didn't expect to be walking down the aisle of a church, wearing a tux and holding a tarantula in my bare hand either. Or hiding under a kitchen table in my underwear.

While we drove to the airport, I thought about Dad and his new family. I figured they'd ask me to come and visit pretty soon. Maybe things would go better the next time. Maybe I could talk to Joan without feeling like a dope. Maybe Hannah and I could get to be friends.

Maybe. It might happen.

And Tony's right. Why stop there? Maybe we'd all end up a big happy family. And maybe we could all go see Tony and Melvin in their new movie.